To our bravest little daredevils, Bodhi,
Fisher, Crosby & Ryder.

—CP and MD

Copyright © 2021 by Wannaplé LLC
Cover and internal design © 2021 by Sourcebooks
Sourcebooks and the colophon are registered trademarks of Sourcebooks.
All rights reserved.
The characters and events portrayed in this book are fictitious or are used fictitiously. Any similarity to real persons, living or dead, is purely coincidental and not intended by the author.
The full color art for this book was created with dramatic flair in Adobe Illustrator.
Published by Sourcebooks Jabberwocky, an imprint of Sourcebooks Kids
P.O. Box 4410, Naperville, Illinois 60567–4410
(630) 961-3900
sourcebookskids.com
Library of Congress Cataloging-in-Publication Data is on file with the publisher.
Source of Production: Leo Paper, Heshan City, Guangdong Province, China
Date of Production: May 2021
Run Number: 5021851
Printed and bound in China.
LEO 10 9 8 7 6 5 4 3 2 1

BOOKS of GREAT CHARACTER

BRAVE LIKE ME

A Story about Finding Your Courage

Words by

CHRISTINE PECK
& MAGS DEROMA

Pictures by

MAGS DEROMA

sourcebooks
jabberwocky

This is Wyatt.

He's got pointy claws on the ends of his giant paws,

which are attached to a particularly large rest-of-his-body.

Looking sharp!

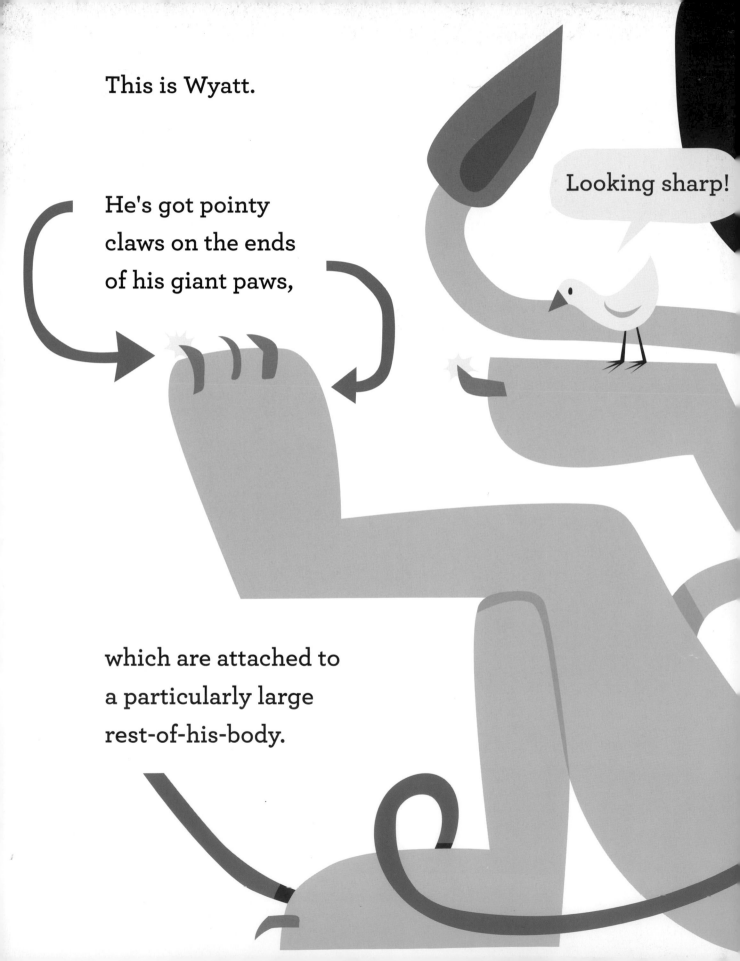

RAWWWRR

He also has a very BIG mouth out of which he can *RAWWWRRRR* extremely loudly.

All of this adds up to one thing: Wyatt is a lion.

And as everyone knows, lions are brave.

So brave!

Ask anyone and they'll tell you that Wyatt is not afraid of aaaaannnnnything.

Spiders?

Nope.

Monsters under the bed?

He scares THEM!

Nope, Wyatt is not afraid of anything, not a single thing.

Oh, Wyatt! We're having a talent show at the theater today. Will you perform?
TALENT SHOW TODAY!
TALENT SHOW TODAY!

Before Wyatt could muster an answer, there was a huge gust of wind, and Pip's hat flew off into the sky!

Without hesitation, Wyatt took off after it.

Don't worry, Pip, I will save it!

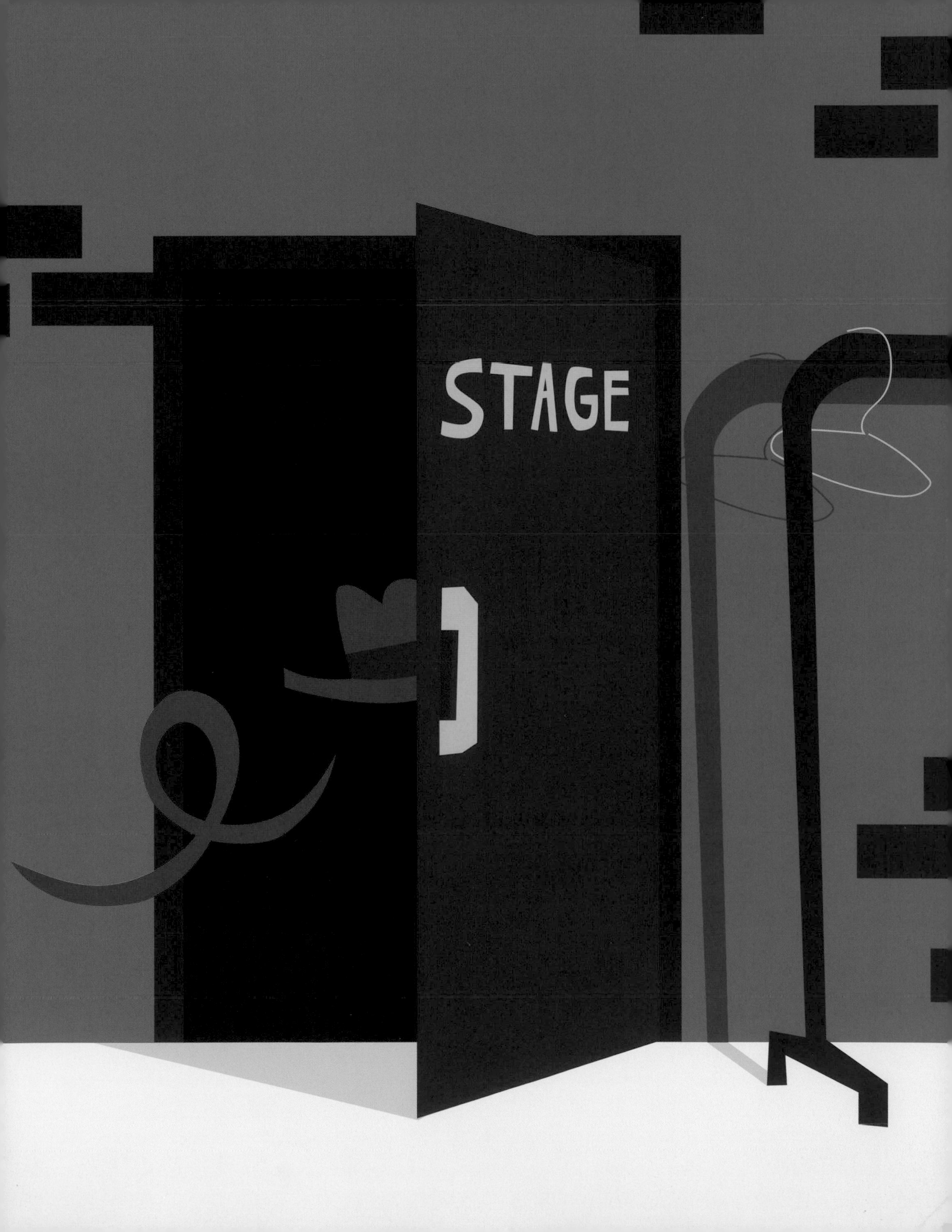
STAGE

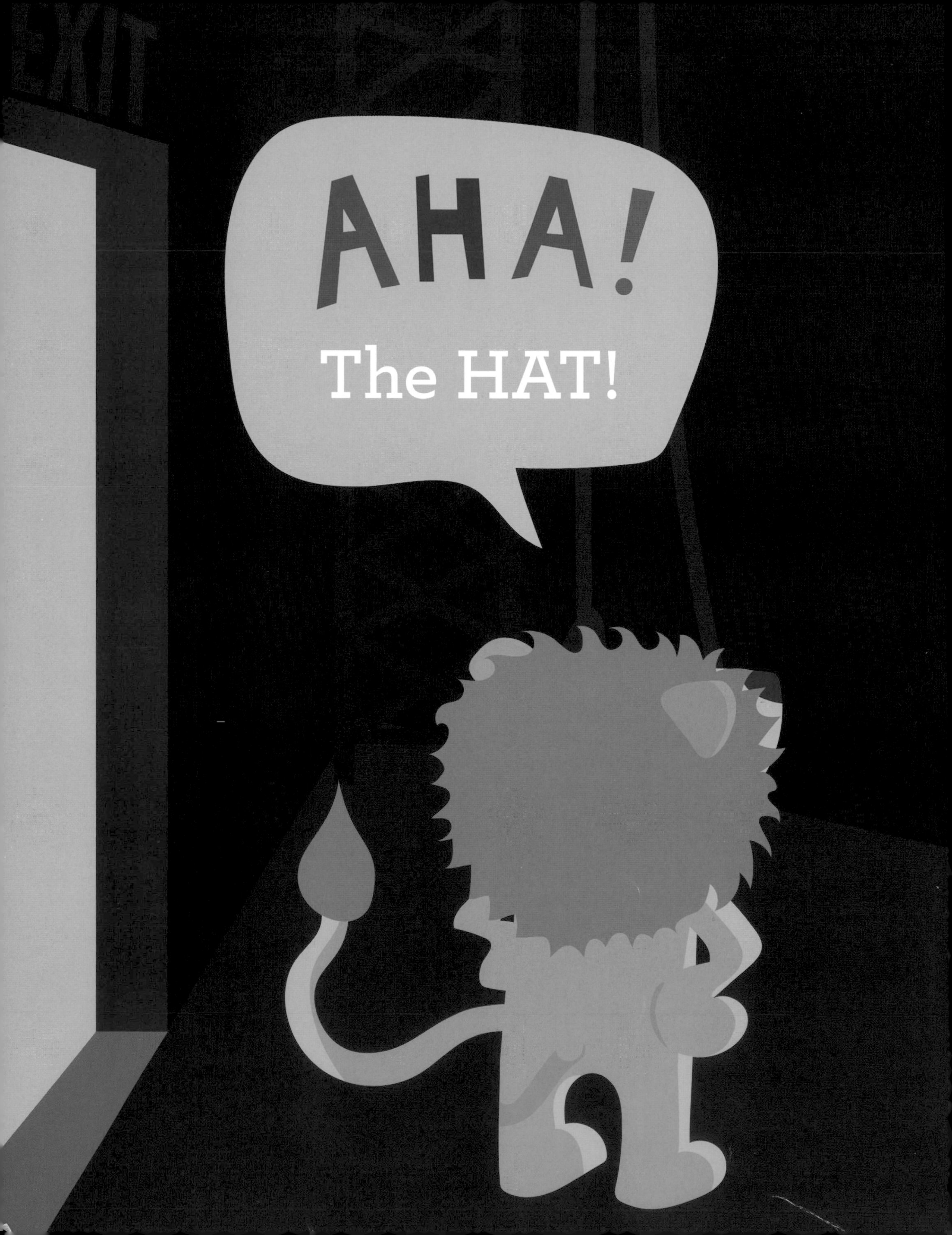
AHA!
The HAT!

Oh dear, Wyatt is freaked out and frozen on stage.

Let's help him be brave.

Everyone, join me in a slow clap!

CLAP!

CLAP!

CLAP!

Everyone! (You too!)

CLAP!

CLAP!

CLAP!

CLAP!

CLAP!

CLAP!

CLAP! CLAP!

CLAP!

CLAP!

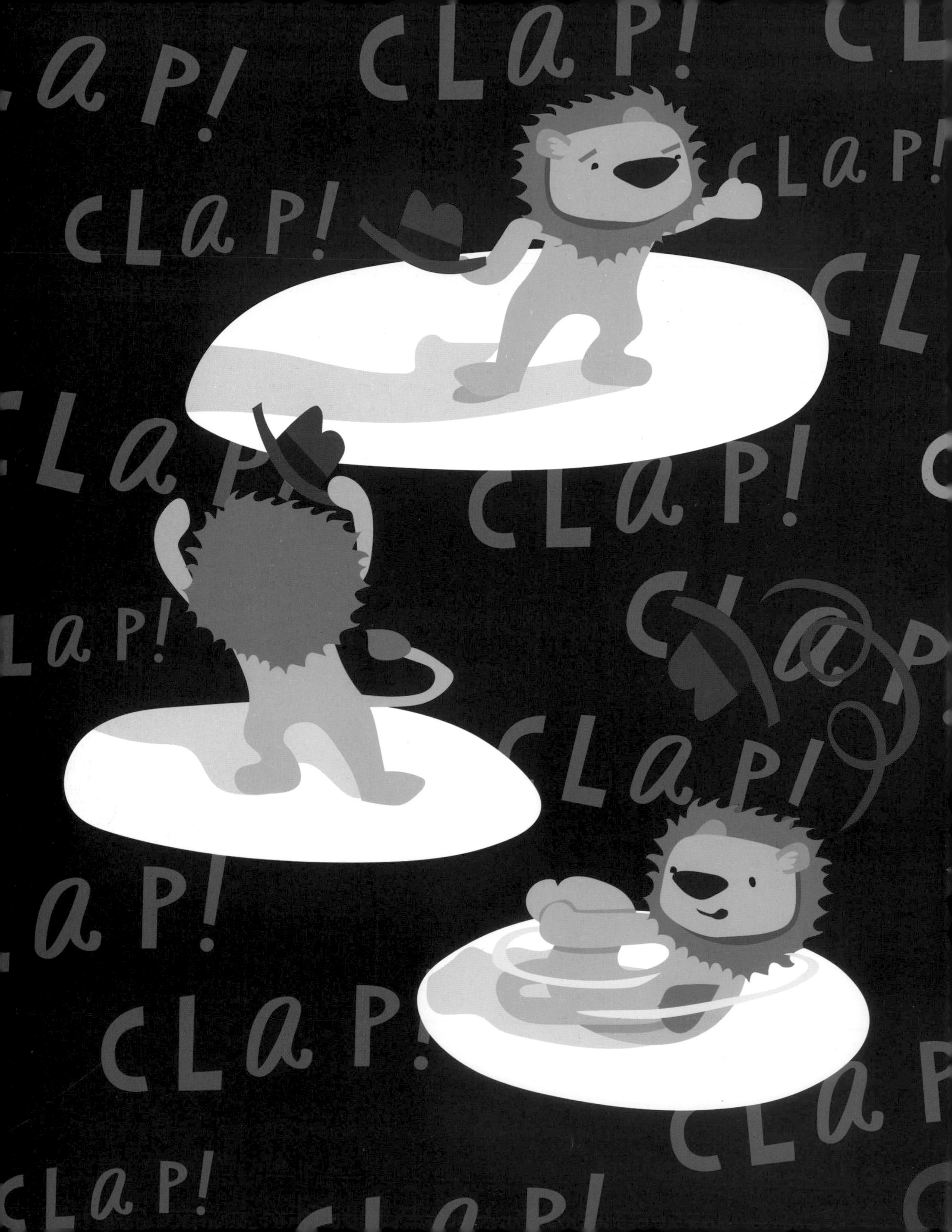
CLAP!
CLAP!
CLAP!
CLAP!
CLAP!
CLAP!

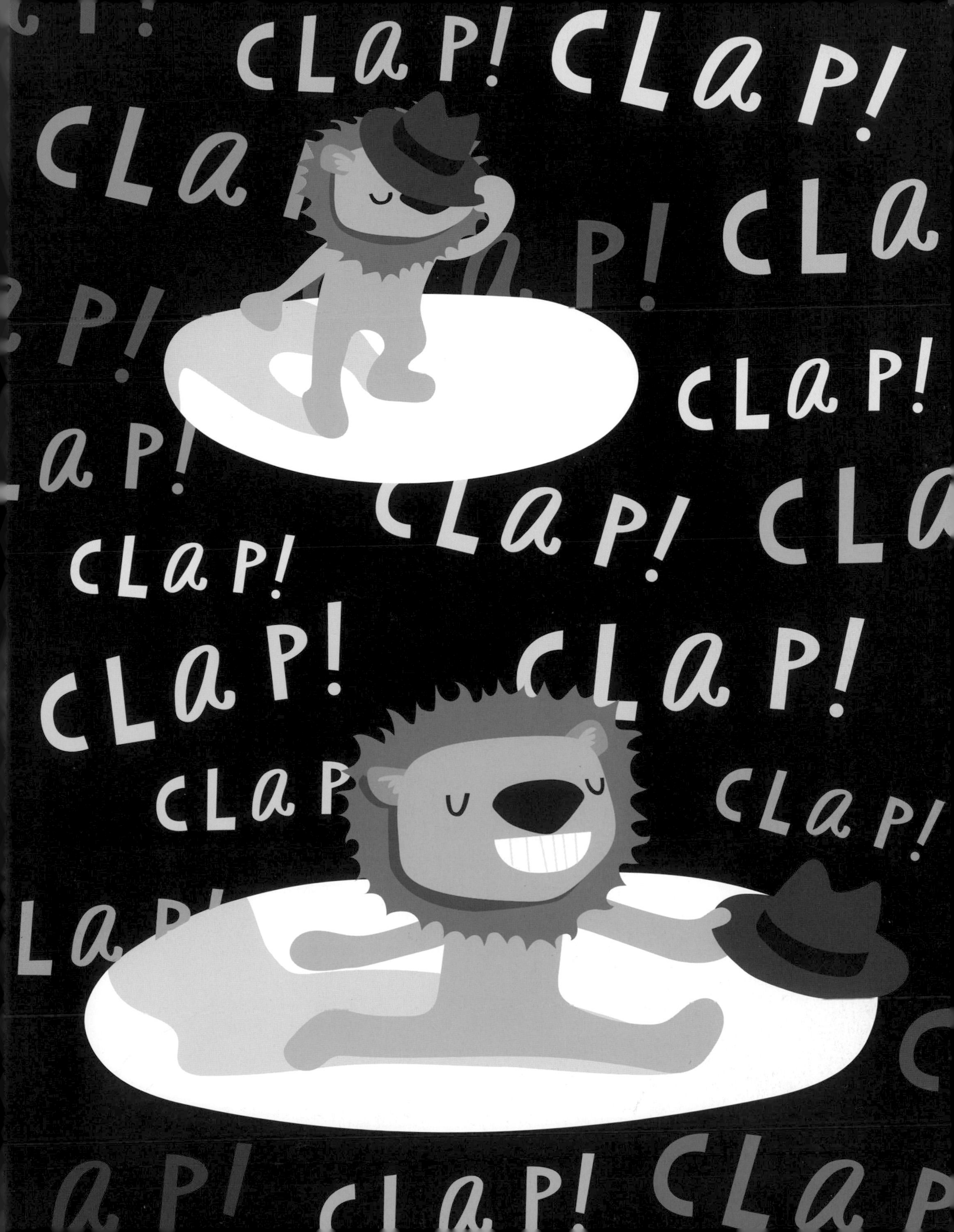
CLAP!
CLAP!
CLAP!
CLAP!
CLAP!
CLAP!
CLAP!
CLAP!
CLAP!

Like I said, everyone knows that lions are brave.

And then the crowd went wild!

SO, YOU WANT to BE BRAVE

In the story you just read, Wyatt the lion was able to face his fear of performing in order to help a friend. Being brave isn't easy, but it is a choice for all of us. Helping to build our confidence and the confidence of those around us makes us believe in ourselves.

BRaveRy

The adventurous and courageous approach to new or uncomfortable experiences.

But how do we help our kiddos build it?

a LITTLe BRAVE

Start small! Bravery is something you can work on in little bits that build up over time. Look for small situations where if feels a *little* less scary to be brave (but where you still *need* to be brave) so you can practice.

A jump off a diving board, ordering your own meal at a restaurant, or speaking up when your ideas are different are some small and approachable ways kiddos can begin to step out of their comfort zone and start to build bravery.

That built-up bravery will show up when they need it most.

SO. MUCH. DRAMA.

Dramatic play is a marvelous way to build bravery. From simply acting out a made-up story as it unfolds to a full-on theatrical premiere, thinking on your feet (and getting a few giggles while you do it) encourages kids to build *adaptability*, bravery's awesome sidekick.

Tell this STORY together: What if _____ could _____?

WHAT'S NEW?

Navigating the new and being brave *together* makes being brave a little more doable (though, not always easier!).

TRY THIS:

Weird (but FUN!) Food Wednesdays – Try a new food you have never tasted, or cook a recipe using an unfamiliar ingredient.

Hometown Tourist – Look at your town through the eyes of a tourist...where could you go or what could you do that you have never done before?

Wandering Way Home – Rather than take the normal route somewhere, try a winding route, and see what new places, sights, or sounds you encounter on the new path.

Eat a New Way – Trying eating with your other hand. It seems silly, but using our bodies to do something normal in an unusual way builds adaptability.

a VOTE for CONFIDENCE!

When kids believe in themselves, they have super powers. Confidence is a big part of bravery. There are loads of ways to help kids be confident. Praise kids for TRYING over completion or success. Model confidence. Give them 15 minutes of totally present alone-time with just you.

TRY THESE FIVE QUICK CONFIDENCE BOOSTERS:

Stand like a superhero!

Get a BIG HUG from someone you love.

Dance like crazy to your favorite song.

Name 5 things you are AWESOME at.

High five yourself in the mirror (gently, of course!).

Silly Street

Silly Street is on a mission to help kids build character through play. Books of Great Character are just one part of our playful character-building world of activities & resources. For more, visit:

PlaySillyStreet.com

you ARe

THan

BRAVER

YOU KNOW

SO, SO BRAVE
SO, SO BRAVE
SO, SO BRAVE
SO, SO BRAVE
SO, SO BRAVE
SO, SO BRAVE